W9-BGM-243

COREY ANN HAYDU

HAND-ME-DOWN
MAGIC

MYSTERIOUS TEA SET

illustrated by
LUiSA URiBE

 KATHERINE TEGEN BOOKS
An Imprint of HarperCollins *Publishers*

ALSO BY COREY ANN HAYDU

Hand-Me-Down Magic #1:
Stoop Sale Treasure

Hand-Me-Down Magic #2:
Crystal Ball Fortunes

Hand-Me-Down Magic #3:
Perfect Patchwork Purse

Katherine Tegen Books is an imprint of HarperCollins Publishers.

Hand-Me-Down Magic #4: Mysterious Tea Set
Text copyright © 2022 by Corey Ann Haydu
Illustrations copyright © 2022 by Luisa Uribe

Library of Congress Control Number: 2021941527
ISBN 978-0-06-287831-1 — ISBN 978-0-06-297828-8 (pbk)

Typography by David DeWitt
21 22 23 24 25 PC/LSCH 10 9 8 7 6 5 4 3 2 1
❖
First Edition

To Mabel Hsu, for your sense of magic,
mystery, wonder, and fun.
To all the people in our lives who help us
remember those things matter.

ALMA'S FAMILY LIVES HERE WITH MANY FLAVORS OF TEA AND PERHAPS SOME HIDDEN MAGIC →

HOME TO TITI ROSA, EVIE, AND THE MOST CROWDED CUPBOARD IMAGINABLE →

DEL'S HOME AND A GREAT PLACE TO DO SERIOUS DETECTIVE WORK →

ABUELITA AND HER SECRETS LIVE HERE →

THE CURIOUS COUSINS SECONDHAND SHOPPE (AT LEAST THREE TEA SETS INSIDE!) →

86 ½
TWENTY-THIRD
AVENUE

A MARVELOUS GARDEN
FOR A TEA PARTY PICNIC

1

Better Than a Gnome

- Del -

On Saturday, the Curious Cousins Secondhand Shoppe was so busy that Del, Alma, and Evie could hardly take a breath. There was a family of five who all wanted purple winter coats, a teenage boy looking for a record player, and of course the woman with the tall red boots and long blue hair, who came every weekend and stayed for hours, picking up and putting down objects, only to ever buy something tiny and random—a thimble, a unicorn figurine, a handful of silver buttons.

Del was in charge of asking customers if they needed any help. One customer was looking for a cuckoo clock, but she cared very much about what sort of cuckoo noise the clock made. Del spent part of the morning helping her test the cuckoos. Another customer wanted to know if they had any hats. Of course, the Curious Cousins Secondhand Shoppe had a great many hats, so Del searched high and low for every last one. After trying on dozens of hats, the customer decided on a pair of mittens instead. Del enjoyed helping with every strange and impossible request, and she thought she had the best job.

Alma was in charge of making change when a customer paid with cash. She was getting very good at math. Evie was in charge of greeting customers. She did it so loudly that Del either cringed or laughed every time a new person came through the door.

Right before lunch, Evie startled a man in a flowered shirt by saying her loudest hello ever. He almost ran right out the door until Abuelita asked what he was looking for.

"A tea set," he said.

"Oh," Abuelita said. She blinked too many times and took too long a pause. "A tea set. I'm sure we have some. I don't care for them much myself. Del, go look for some tea sets for our customer, okay?" Del had never heard Abuelita comment on a customer's request before. In fact, she'd always told Del that wasn't their job. That's why Del just smiled and said, "Sure, let me look!" when someone asked for things she didn't like— itchy sweaters and uncomfortable couches and scary books.

"Tea sets coming right up!" Del said, just like Abuelita had taught her. She knew there was a pink tea set on the shelf by a box of old postcards and a yellow tea set with some broken parts over by the rocking horse. Del walked the aisles

3

looking for more hidden tea sets. There weren't any by the collection of fancy coats, and there weren't any in the furniture section either. Del knelt to the ground in the jewelry section. It was one of her favorite places to spend time—with glittering stones and heavy chains and elaborate brooches featuring every imaginable animal and flower.

Del moved a few jewelry boxes aside. When she moved the heaviest, fanciest jewelry box, she found it. A very beautiful tea set. This, she was sure, would be the one the man picked. It looked delicate and sweet, with green-and-blue designs on it. She was a little sad, actually, that she'd have to say goodbye to this tea set only moments after discovering it.

She brought all the tea sets to the front of the store, where the man was enjoying some of Abuelita's homemade gofio. He poured the sugary-sweet powdered candy right into his mouth, and a little bit of it dusted his face.

"I found three tea sets," Del said, placing each one gingerly in front of the man.

"Bien hecho, Del," Abuelita said. She was always complimenting Del on her object-finding abilities. There was never a disappointed customer at Curious Cousins.

The man and his powdery gofio fingers picked up pieces of each tea set. And to Del's delight, he shook his head when he picked up the beautiful blue-and-green teapot of Del's favorite set. "My kids really prefer pink," he said. "I'll take the pink one."

Del thought the pink one was sort of boring compared to the blue-and-green one, but she happily carried it to the counter for him anyway.

"BIENVENIDOS!" Evie said, way too loudly, welcoming a family of four who had just walked through the door. "Everything in the store is ten percent off this week, so you should get way more than you planned, okay? We have a very nice collection of garden gnomes today. And there's even a chandelier in the back! Want me to show you?"

"Oh, um, we're okay!" one of the new customers said, clearly flustered by Evie's excitement. "We're not really looking for gnomes. Or a chandelier."

Del and Alma exchanged a glance. No matter how many times Abuelita told Evie what to say to customers—*exactly* what to say to them—Evie always found a way to make it her own.

"Gnomes, huh?" the man with the pink tea set said before handing his money over to Alma. "Maybe I'd be interested in some gnomes. I'll leave this here and be right back, okay?"

"No problem," Alma said. She and Del were having trouble holding in their laughter. Evie was absolutely beaming.

"Let's go!" Evie said, bouncing up and down a little. "There are big gnomes and little gnomes and a few in-between ones too, but big or little is probably better, don't you think?"

"I guess so," the man said, following now-galloping Evie to the gnome section of the store.

Finally, Del and Alma could collapse into giggles. "She's going to sell every gnome in the store by the end of the day," Del said.

"And a chandelier!" Alma exclaimed. She looked at the tea set the man had set down. "This is pretty."

"Don't worry—he didn't choose the really

cool tea set," Del said. "I'll show you after he leaves, okay?"

Alma nodded. The man came back with three gnomes, one tiny one and two truly enormous ones. Evie helped him carry them all, plus his pink tea set, to his car outside.

"Enjoy the gnomes!" Evie said.

"Enjoy the tea set!" Del said.

"Enjoy your day!" Alma said.

Finally, it was lunchtime.

But better than lunchtime, it was very nearly time for Del to show Alma her new favorite object in the Curious Cousins Secondhand Shoppe. Del could hardly wait.

2

A Little Lost, a Little Broken

-Alma-

After about ten minutes of tidying up, Alma caught sight of her friend June and June's abuela outside the window. June had very curly brown hair and a very big smile and always carried her favorite doll around the neighborhood. The doll had at least a dozen fancy outfits that Alma just loved.

Alma waved her hand excitedly. June had a huge imagination, so it was always fun to play

9

with her and her doll. One time they pretended they were astronauts going to Pluto to have a birthday party with aliens. Another time they pretended that June's doll was going to the White House to have a very important meeting with the president about making summer vacation longer.

"June! Come have lunch with us!" Alma called out through the open window.

"Oh! Fun!" June said. But June's abuela shook her head.

"Not today, June," she said. Her voice was quiet and a little sad. Alma noticed she was wearing a sparkly headband and shimmery eye shadow. She wondered if maybe June's abuela was as magical as her own.

"But Abuelita's going to make sandwiches!" Alma said. "Right, Abuelita?"

Abuelita looked up from the counter she was wiping off to see June and her abuela and Alma's eager face.

"Oh. Well. I'm not sure I have enough turkey

for everyone, actually. Or bread. We're low on bread, Alma." Abuelita was mumbling. Abuelita never mumbled.

"We are?" Alma asked, puzzled. Outside the window, June looked puzzled too.

"Well then, it's settled. Hasta luego, Alma," June's abuela said, though it didn't seem like she wanted to see them later. In fact, she mostly looked relieved. She fluttered her fingers in a very pretty, ballerina-like goodbye.

"See ya," June said. The girls waved goodbye, too, not quite as gracefully, both shrugging their shoulders with confusion.

"Abuelita, I'm sure we could have figured out a way to make lunch for June."

"Ah, well, next time," Abuelita said. "I'll be right back with our sandwiches, bueno?"

"Okay," Alma said. She didn't have time to dwell on the funny exchange, because as soon as Abuelita was gone, Del pulled Alma and Evie over to the blue-and-green tea set.

"Look!" she said. "Isn't it gorgeous?"

Alma picked up the teapot. Evie picked up the saucer. "It's pretty," Alma said, a little confused, "but where are the cups?" There were eight little plates but only one tiny chipped cup. Alma knew that when Del got excited, it was possible for her to miss almost anything. When Del found an orange sweater with llamas on it at the store last week, she was so excited she didn't notice it was three sizes too big. When she got excited about the cake she was baking for Abuelita's birthday, she forgot to put in the sugar. And when she tried to tell Alma about a book she loved, she forgot the names of all the characters.

"Oh," Del said. "That's strange."

"Very strange," Alma said.

"Mysterious," Evie said, because Evie had just learned the word *mysterious* and liked to say it while wiggling her eyebrows.

Alma leaned in. "Still, it's really pretty," she said. "What's painted on it?" She leaned in even closer. She blinked. "Wait. Del. Is that . . ."

Del looked closer too. "It's a tree," she said.

"Doesn't it look sort of like—" Alma began.

"The sobbing willow!" Evie interrupted so loudly Alma was sure the glass kitten figurines behind them almost shattered.

"Our sobbing willow?" Del asked.

"No way," Alma said, shaking her head. But it was very clear that the thing painted on each

piece of the tea set was their favorite neighborhood tree. The tree that was planted right down the street, that they could see from their very own window. The tree they called the sobbing willow, for how far down its branches drooped.

"I can't believe it!" Alma said.

"Can't believe what, mi cielo?" Abuelita asked, coming back into the store with four sandwiches.

"Our sobbing willow is on this tea set!" Alma said. "Do you know where it came from? Or why it's here? Or why it's missing most of its cups?"

"Someone from the neighborhood must have made it, right?" Del asked. "Was it Cassie's mom? She's really artsy. Or maybe Felix painted it? He loves that tree."

"Can we make tea?" Evie interrupted. "I've never had tea. Can we put sugar in it? I want to have a tea party! Can Oscar come? And Fraidy-cat?"

"The tea set is—it's complicated," Abuelita said at last.

"Is it magical?" Del asked. Del thought almost everything was magical, and maybe she was right.

Abuelita shrugged. "I haven't seen it in many years. It's not the sort of thing— Some things belong in the past. Even magical things. And besides, magic only works when nothing is lost or broken."

Alma looked at Del and Del looked back. Abuelita always said they had the Curious

Cousins shop because the past should never be lost. What she was saying didn't make any sense at all.

"So this tea set *is* magical?" Del asked.

Abuelita gave a not-very-Abuelita shrug. She looked sad. "If it ever was," she said, "it's certainly not now."

"But—" Del started, her eyes sparkling with thoughts of magic.

"Please put it away. I don't want to look at it right now. No one will want to buy a tea set with missing cups anyway," Abuelita said.

"I want it!" Evie said.

"No," Abuelita said. "And that's final."

Abuelita walked away from the girls, heading to the back of the store. Alma had a million questions. But it was obvious that Abuelita didn't want to answer any of them.

Alma and Del exchanged glances.

"I'll bring it up to my bedroom," Del whispered.

Alma knew she should maybe say no. But

Abuelita wanted the tea set to be somewhere that she didn't have to look at it. And she'd said herself that no one would want to buy it. So it was just fine to bring it up to Del's room instead of putting it on a high shelf somewhere in the store.

Right?

"Good idea," Alma said. Except she wasn't totally sure that it was.

3

The Best Place to Start

- Del -

Del and Alma climbed the stairs of 86 ½ Twenty-Third Avenue as soon as Abuelita told them they were free to go. They ran the whole way and were breathless with excitement and nervousness by the time they arrived at Del's bedroom.

Evie was joining them, too, but she got distracted by the smell of pernil wafting out of her family's home. Evie loved the slow-cooked pork more than any other meal their family made. She couldn't resist getting an early bite of her favorite dinner. Del was a little bit relieved. She and Alma had serious work to do, trying to solve the mystery of the tea set. And Evie had a habit of distracting them.

"Well, here it is," Del said, placing the tea set on her bed. Alma looked nervous. She didn't touch the tea set at all.

"Maybe this was a mistake," she said. "Abuelita said—"

"Abuelita said she didn't want to see it anymore. And now she can't see it. Stop worrying." Del flipped every one over and looked at the bottom of each tiny plate for clues about who made them—a signature maybe? Even initials? But all Del could find was a tiny heart painted on the bottom of the cup.

"Maybe the heart is a clue?" she said.

"A clue for what?" Alma asked.

"For solving the mystery of the tea set! Where it came from and why Abuelita doesn't like it and where all the missing cups are!"

"Maybe we're not supposed to know any of that," Alma said. "Abuelita just told us that some things should stay in the past."

Del shook her head. "A mystery is meant to be solved," she said. "That's what makes it a mystery! So let's see. A heart. A heart means love, right? So this tea set was made with love."

"I guess so," Alma said.

"And the missing cups mean something went wrong. A tea set shouldn't have missing cups." Del liked trying to solve a mystery. She wondered if maybe she would make a good detective someday.

"That's true," Alma said. "Maybe that means we shouldn't be playing with it?"

Del needed Alma to stop worrying and start helping if she was going to solve this mystery. Detectives needed partners. "No way," Del said. "It means we have to find the other teacups!"

"Oh," Alma said. "But Abuelita said—"

"We won't talk to her about it!" Del said.

"That's what she wanted. Stop worrying, Alma."

"The tea set made Abuelita really sad," Alma said quietly. "What if us trying to solve the mystery makes her even sadder?"

Del shook her head. "Look at this heart. Abuelita says that nothing matters more than love. And these teacups have something to do with love. I'm positive."

Alma sighed. Del sighed back.

"But what if—?" Alma started.

"What if Abuelita's sad because she misses the other teacups? What if finding them for her would actually make her happy? We have to at least try," Del said. She watched as Alma thought about what she was saying. Alma's face went from very worried to a little less worried to maybe a tiny bit interested.

"Where would teacups made with love *be*?" Alma asked. "They're probably in the neighborhood, right? Because of the sobbing willow?"

Del grinned.

"Yes," she said, nodding her head and stroking her chin. She had seen many detectives on TV, and they all nodded their heads and stroked their chins. They knit their brows too. She tried that.

"Are you okay?" Alma asked. "You look funny."

Del unknit her eyebrows. Maybe she wasn't quite ready for that yet.

"Well," Del said, "there's nowhere in the world with more love than 86 ½ Twenty-Third Avenue, right?"

"I guess that's true," Alma said.

Del didn't know much about teacups or how to knit her eyebrows together the right way, but she knew a lot about love and a lot about this building. "So if the teacups were made with love, maybe they're all here."

"All here with our family?" Alma asked.

"Maybe!" Del said. Then she decided a detective needed to be surer of herself. "Probably! Let's go look."

"Where should we start?" Alma asked. "In someone's cupboard, I guess?"

Del nodded and stroked her chin. "The cupboards! Yes. The perfect place to find a missing teacup. I think we need to start with Titi Rosa's cupboards."

"Why Titi Rosa?" Alma asked.

Del dropped her voice into a low whisper.

It seemed like the kind of voice a very serious detective might use. "The tea set has something to do with love and something to do with Abuelita."

"Okay . . . ," Alma said.

"Titi Rosa is Abuelita's best friend," Del said, "and they really love each other. So it just makes sense to start with her. That's what the clues are leading to."

Alma looked a little unsure. She would probably take a little longer to trust her detective instincts. Del would have to help her. "Trust me," Del said. "We have to start with Abuelita's best friend."

Alma gave a little smile and nodded. "Best friends are always the best place to start," she declared.

Del smiled back. "I couldn't agree more."

4

A Question That Is Meant to Be Answered

-Alma-

Alma and Del walked up one flight of stairs to get to Titi Rosa's kitchen. They walked right in as always, and as always Titi Rosa greeted them both with enormous hugs and offers for all kinds of food.

Evie was at the counter drawing a picture of the sobbing willow and perked right up seeing her older cousins. "Oh good, you're here!" she said. "I have a lot of ideas for what to do with the tea set. We should make our own teacups for it. And then we should have a tea party with everyone in the neighborhood or at least all our stuffed animals. And we should serve hot chocolate instead of tea. And put chocolate syrup in the creamer. And put chocolate chips in the sugar bowl. Okay?"

Alma smiled. And she had to admit, Evie's idea did sound pretty delicious. And maybe a little less scary than trying to solve a mystery she wasn't sure they should be trying to solve. "Maybe, Evie," she said.

"Well, I'm practicing my tree-drawing to pre-pare," Evie said. She showed them her sobbing willow drawing. It was a little lopsided and a little too big for the paper, but it was also pretty good. Was it a clue that Evie was good at drawing sobbing willows? Alma wasn't sure, but she suddenly felt a bit more like a detective. She looked at Del and tried to say with her eyes, *Let's discuss this later.* Del looked back, and Alma was pretty sure she was saying, *Yes, we will discuss this and many other clues later.*

"Now, girls," Titi Rosa said. "I know Abuelita doesn't like anyone using that tea set. But I'd be happy to get you a new tea set of your very own. Bueno?"

Alma wanted to say yes, that was fine, that was probably a good idea. But Del had other plans.

"No, that's not good," Del said. "We need this tea set."

"What I think Del means," Alma said, "is that we really love the sobbing-willow tea set, and we're sad that the cups are missing, and I guess we're hoping maybe we could find them and make the set whole again." Titi Rosa tapped her foot and crossed her arms. "We thought maybe the teacups being missing were part of what was making Abuelita so sad."

"Well. Hmm. I don't know about that," Titi Rosa said.

"Can we just look in your cupboard?" Del asked. "Maybe there's one of the teacups there?"

Titi Rosa tapped her finger against the counter. That's what she did when she was thinking. She tapped for a long, long time, so she must be having a *lot* of big thoughts.

"Mysteries are meant to be solved, I suppose," Titi Rosa said at last, just like Del had said. "Maybe your abuelita is finally ready for this one to be solved."

Alma felt a little bit less nervous. If Titi Rosa said it was okay, maybe it really was.

"I want to look too!" Evie said when Del and

Alma walked over to the cupboard. "I'm really good at looking for things!"

"Next time," Del said. "This is very serious work for very serious detectives."

Evie pouted while Del opened the cupboard door. Inside were more cups and plates and bowls and platters than Alma would have ever imagined.

It took a while, but Alma, Del, and even little Evie carefully took out every last object in Titi Rosa's cupboard. There were square plates and circular plates and tall glasses and tiny doll-sized ones. There were brightly colored bowls and plain white bowls. But Alma didn't see any teacups.

"I guess we'll have to try somewhere else," she said as Del took out the last few objects.

"Wait!" Del said. "Wait, I think it's here!" Del scrunched up her face and reached her whole arm into the cupboard. She grunted with effort. "I think—yep, here it is! I got it!"

And with that, Del pulled out one single perfect teacup that perfectly matched the sobbing-willow tea set.

"Titi Rosa, why do you have this?" Alma asked excitedly.

Titi Rosa looked happy-sad. Or maybe sad-happy. "Some questions have been left unanswered too long, I think," she said. "And perhaps that's all I should say for now."

Alma and Del looked at each other. Del stroked her chin. Alma raised her eyebrows. Evie tried to grab the cup.

Alma scrunched her toes. This mystery was clearly a very big, very important one.

And that made Alma very nervous.

5

As Much Magic as Everyone Else

- Del -

"Can we take this with us?" Del asked Titi Rosa. "We'll be very careful with it."

"Oh, girls. It's a big responsibility," Titi Rosa said nervously. She and Abuelita were best friends but also very different, just like Del and Alma. Abuelita liked things to be neat and orderly. Titi Rosa's home was always a bit of a mess. Abuelita spoke very carefully, and always sounded wise and certain. Titi Rosa spoke quickly and laughed often and didn't ever say much about magic.

Abuelita was a calming presence, and Titi Rosa was the life of the party. Del was so happy they were both in her family. Every family needed both sides.

"Please, Titi?" Del said. She fluttered her eyelashes. Alma clasped her hands in front of her chest, begging.

"Welllllll," Titi Rosa said. "You can *borrow* it, okay? Solamente borrow. I expect you to bring it back soon."

"Of course!" Alma said.

"Thank you so much!" Del said.

"And maybe don't tell your abuelita," Titi Rosa whispered. "For now, at least." Titi Rosa gave a secret smile—pursed lips, bright eyes, raised eyebrows.

"Where are the rest of the teacups?" Del asked Titi Rosa. Titi Rosa's secret smile grew.

"Oh, they went this way and that. They went away. But not too far," Titi Rosa said.

"What does that mean?" Alma asked. It sounded like a riddle, and Alma had never been very good at riddles.

"It means we don't always need to go far away to get what we need. We just need to go deeper in. We need to get to the bottom of things." Titi Rosa raised her eyebrows. But she didn't give them time to ask any more questions. She told them something about needing to iron her curtains and that maybe she'd said too much, and she shooed them out the door.

Alma, Del, and Evie brought the teacup to Del's room, but there were still six teacups missing.

"We don't need to go far," Del said, repeating Titi Rosa's words to see if she could make them make sense.

"We need to go deep," Alma finished. "We need to get to the bottom of things."

"The bottom of things," Del repeated a few times, turning the teacup over and over in her hands.

"The bottom of things!" Alma exclaimed. "Maybe there's something on the bottom of this teacup too!"

Del turned the cup over. And sure enough, there was a pink rose painted onto the bottom of the cup, just like the heart on the bottom of the other cup. Alma beamed with pride. Maybe she wasn't so nervous anymore about solving the mystery.

"I guess we go to the rose garden?" Del said.

"Those roses aren't pink," Evie chimed in.

Del stroked her chin and pursed her lips. That was true. Titi Clara liked red and yellow roses but didn't like pink ones. But there was someone in the family who liked pink roses. There was someone who liked pink roses so much they lined their cabinets and drawers with pink rose paper.

And that someone was Del's mom.

"I know where it is!" Del exclaimed, and she ran to her kitchen, with Alma and Evie following behind.

Del flung open her cabinets to reveal the pink roses lining the inside. Alma gasped. Evie yipped. Del got to work.

They took out all the oatmeal and pasta and olive oil, but finally behind three cans of soup, there was a teacup. Another perfect teacup.

Del grinned. Alma beamed. Evie squealed so loudly Del worried the cup might break. They were real mystery-solving detectives!

"Do you think there's another clue?" Alma asked.

Del took a deep breath before turning the cup over. And there, right on the bottom of the cup was what must be another clue. A purple rectangle. No one said anything. They just thought and thought and thought. Mysteries, it turned out, were a little like magic. Exciting and strange and hard to understand.

"Where is there a purple rectangle?" Alma asked.

"Our door is purple," Evie said. Del's heart raced. That was true. But it didn't help very much. 86 ½ Twenty-Third Avenue was pretty big. There must be another purple rectangle in here somewhere. Del's mind spun with ideas.

"Napkins!" Del exclaimed at last. "Alma, you have purple napkins at your home!" She grabbed her cousins' hands and dragged them upstairs to the top floor of the building, where Alma lived.

The girls looked through all the drawers and cabinets and closets until they finally found a box of purple napkins that Alma's mom and dad liked to use for special occasions. Evie dug right in, flinging napkins everywhere. But when she got to the bottom of the box, there was nothing there.

"Oh," Alma said. "There probably aren't any cups at my house anyway."

"Or we just have to look harder!" Del said. She didn't want Alma to give up. Not already! And she certainly didn't want her worried that there wasn't enough magic in her home. Alma was always worried about not being magical enough. Del hoped and hoped and hoped that there was a mysterious teacup hidden somewhere on the top floor to prove her wrong. And she would look as hard as she needed to find it.

"Let's just go to Titi Clara's," Alma said. "Or maybe Uncle Andy's. I bet they have cups there."

Del could tell Alma was starting to feel sorry for herself. "You have just as much magic as the rest of us," Del said. "I'm sure of it. We just have to keep trying to think of where purple rectangles might be." Alma half-heartedly looked in her parents' dresser and in the washing machine. But Del went right to Alma's bedroom.

"No one would put a teacup in a bedroom," Alma called after her. "It's not in there."

"That's what you think!" Del said. She looked everywhere. In her desk drawers and behind the curtains. Under her pile of stuffed animals and in her sock drawer. No purple rectangles. No teacups. Finally, Del opened up Alma's closet. She sorted through her dresses and looked on the shelves. No teacup. Del frowned. She knelt on the ground and started pushing aside Alma's shoes. There, in the back corner of the closet, behind sneakers and ballet slippers and flip-flops, was a shoebox. Del smiled. The shoebox looked a little tired and a little smushed. But all that really mattered was that it was purple.

A purple rectangle.

"Alma, come here!" she called. When Alma came in, she looked very skeptical, but Del didn't mind. "Look!" she said.

"A purple rectangle? In my own closet?" Alma said. She sounded surprised. And confused. And a little bit excited too. She took a deep breath and nudged the top of the box open. When she saw what was inside, she gasped. The fourth teacup!

"I knew it," Del said.

"I didn't," Alma said. She cradled the cup in her hand.

"Where are the rest?" Evie asked. "How many more are there?"

"Four more," Del said. "I guess we better keep going."

"We'll find them all!" Alma said. Del had never heard her cousin more determined. And she really, really liked it.

6

Everything's a Mystery

-Alma-

Alma knew just what to do with the teacup. She turned it right over, knowing that there would be a clue on the back, like magic.

And there it was. A solid white circle.

Del thought it was a cracker.

"It's the moon," Evie said confidently. "We're going to have to go to the moon! I'm hungry. Do they have cookies on the moon?" It took Del and Alma a while to talk Evie out of her moon travel plan. They came up with some other ideas—maybe the white circle was just a white plate. But everyone had white plates. And everyone had crackers. Those weren't very good clues.

"What else is white and round?" Del asked nobody in particular.

Alma closed her eyes and thought and thought and thought. "A baseball!" she said at last.

Del looked at her cousin. Evie looked at the sky, still thinking about the moon, maybe.

"Doesn't Uncle Andy love baseball?" Alma said. "Maybe the next teacup is at his home."

"You're a genius!" Del said, and the girls paraded to Uncle Andy's building a few doors down.

"We need your baseballs!" Evie declared to a very confused Uncle Andy when they arrived.

"We're looking for something special, and we think maybe it's with your baseballs," Alma explained.

"My baseballs?" Uncle Andy asked, furrowing his brow. "I don't really have any baseballs."

"You don't?" Alma asked. She thought she might cry. Her genius idea wasn't very good after all. "I thought you loved baseball."

"I do," Uncle Andy said. "But I don't have any balls. I do have a lot of baseball cards! Would that help?"

Alma's heart lifted again. "Yes! That might work!"

Uncle Andy showed them the six big boxes he kept his cards in, and in no time at all they'd

found the fifth teacup. Alma hugged it to her chest. She was especially proud of finding this one.

"Can we have this?" Del called out to her uncle.

"Not if it's Roberto Clemente," Uncle Andy answered without looking up to see what they were holding.

"Who's Roberto Clemente?" Evie asked with wide eyes. Evie was curious about absolutely

everything. Even things she knew nothing about.

"Well, let me tell you—" Uncle Andy began, but Alma shook her head and laughed.

"We aren't actually taking a baseball card," Alma said. "It's this teacup." She held the fifth sobbing-willow teacup up for him to see. He squinted. And then—Alma was pretty sure even though it made no sense—Uncle Andy *blushed*.

"Oh. That. Huh. I didn't know it was back there. You sure you wouldn't rather talk baseball for a bit? I'll trade you some really good cards for that teacup."

"We don't really collect baseball cards," Alma said.

"We could!" Evie said. "Maybe baseball cards are better than teacups anyway. Maybe baseball cards are magical!"

"They probably are," Del said, leaning down so that she was face-to-face with her cousin.

"But let's do one magical adventure at a time, okay?"

Evie nodded with seriousness. "Yes," she said. "That's smart. We'll be back next week to figure out baseball card magic, Uncle Andy, okay? And then you can tell me about your friend Roberto."

"But for now, could we please have this teacup? And maybe hear where you got it from?" Del asked.

"You can have it," Uncle Andy said, "but I'm afraid I can't tell you much about it. It's, uh, hard to even remember that sort of thing, you know?"

"I guess," Del said.

"Just be careful with it, okay? It's—it's special." Uncle Andy was mumbling.

"That was pretty weird," Alma said as they walked away from Uncle Andy's.

"A mystery," Del agreed.

"Well, time for our next clue," Alma said, turning the cup over. Every time she found a new clue on the bottom of a cup, she was filled with wonder. Somehow, someone had left clues to find magic in the homes of all their family members. And somehow they were able to understand the clues. And somehow, somehow they were finding all the missing teacups and solving the mystery together.

Magic.

This time, on the bottom of the cup was painted the shape of a bird.

"A bird stole the sixth teacup!" Evie exclaimed, looking up into the trees where many birds were chirping.

"I'm not sure that's it, Evie," Del said.

"There are birds everywhere in the neighborhood," Alma said. "What does this mean?"

"Birds live outside," Del said, "so I think we need to visit everyone who has a backyard."

Alma nodded. It was a very good plan. Their walking had brought them right in front of Titi

Clara's bright green door. Titi Clara lived on the first floor, and her children, Titi Selma and Tío Ramon, lived on the second and third floors with their families. They both had brand-new babies, so the girls hadn't seen as much of them lately. Still, Titi Clara welcomed them into the building with a wide grin and told the girls they should visit the whole family.

"We're actually here on a mission," Del said.

"That sounds quite official," Titi Clara said.

"We're detectives," Evie said. "Teacup detectives."

"Teacups?" Titi Clara asked. But Alma could swear her voice was shaking a little.

"Do you know

anything about teacups?" Del asked. She really did sound like a detective. Her voice was serious and low. She crossed her arms over her chest and tilted her chin down. Alma tried to do the same, but it didn't feel quite right on her.

"Ah," Titi Clara said. "Teacups. Have you asked your abuelita about them?" Alma, Del, and Evie nodded. "Some mysteries are meant to remain in the past. Entienden todos?"

Alma shook her head. She did not understand. Why was everyone being so funny about these teacups? And weren't mysteries meant to be solved anyway?

"You may not solve the mystery of where the teacups came from," Titi Clara said slowly. "But I suppose you are welcome to solve the mystery of where they are now."

She nodded in the direction of her backyard, where Titi Selma was working on putting up a swing set.

"In the backyard?" Alma asked. "Why would you keep a teacup in the backyard?"

Titi Clara shrugged. "Maybe that's a mystery too," she said. "Maybe everything we do is a little bit of a mystery, no?"

Alma certainly couldn't disagree with that.

7

Backyard Magic

- Del -

Titi Clara's backyard was nothing like Abuelita's garden, except that it was also magical-looking and perfect to spend an afternoon in.

"Buenos días, girls," Titi Selma said. She was sweating and holding a hammer and looking a little perplexed by all the parts for the swing set.

"Buenos días," Del said. She loved Titi Selma, who was always cracking jokes and telling her stories about the family, about Puerto Rico, and about all the characters on her favorite telenovela. "How are you? How's the baby?"

"Oh, Louise is beautiful and perfect and never sleeps," Titi Selma said. "How are all of you?"

"Well, we're trying to track down some teacups," Del said hopefully. If anyone would know the story of the teacups, it would be Titi Selma.

But Titi Selma only smiled. "Teacups. Well. Not what I thought you'd say. Take a look around."

Everything Del could possibly imagine was in the backyard. A fairy statue. Four different pink bicycles. A fake palm tree covered in Christmas lights. And a dining room table. The girls wandered around, looking under and over everything.

"Oh!" Del said. "Oh, oh, oh! Look at these!" Del was in the far corner of the backyard, away from the swing set and bikes and hammock.

"What'd you find?" Alma asked.

Evie didn't ask anything. And she didn't follow Alma over to Del. She was too focused on helping Titi Selma build the swing set. Evie was holding the directions upside down and looking for a wrench. Del was pretty sure that Evie didn't know what a wrench was, but Titi Selma would figure that out soon enough.

"I found magic," Del said. And when Alma reached her, she had to agree. Del had found a collection of birdcages.

"Birds!" Alma exclaimed, too excited to say anything else.

Some of the birdcages were enormous and white, and some were so small a caterpillar could barely fit inside. Some were decorated with jewels and some with delicate carvings. Others were sturdy and metal and not very pretty at all. But inside each one was a

different mysterious treasure. A small, smooth purple stone. An old brass key. A pouch full of something that smelled delicious. And, in the very last birdcage, which was silvery and skinny and squeaky, there it was. A teacup. A perfect, sobbing-willow, probably magical, definitely mysterious teacup.

And on the bottom was painted a little green Christmas tree.

"Find what you were looking for?" Titi Selma asked distractedly as Del and Alma ran across the lawn.

"Sure did! Can we check out your place next?" Del said.

"You're welcome to, but I don't even drink tea," Titi Selma said.

"We'll see about that," Del whispered to Alma as they went back into the building, leaving Evie behind to keep helping Titi Selma.

8

Babies, Baubles, and Boxes

-Alma-

Titi Selma's apartment was brightly colored and absolutely packed with toys for Baby Louise. There was an oversize teddy bear that seemed to be as big as Alma, a tiny baby-size piano, three boxes of baby books. Plus, there was Baby Louise herself, who was dark-haired and drooly and very, very cute. The girls waved hello to Uncle Marcus and tried to quickly explain what they were up to. He smiled and gave a wave of his hand.

"I know better than to ask questions," he said. "Feel free to look around for any sort of magic you think we have."

"Goooooowah!" Baby Louise agreed.

Alma and Del looked everywhere, but they didn't see any Christmas trees.

"Where do you keep your Christmas decorations?" Alma asked Uncle Marcus.

"Good idea, Alma!" Del exclaimed. Alma beamed. She was getting better and better at being a teacup detective, and she straightened her back and lifted her chin with detective pride.

"Oh, we don't have any here. Tío Ramon is the king of Christmas. He decorates for all of us. Won't let us touch the ornaments or lights or anything," Uncle Marcus said, shaking his head.

"The king of Christmas?" Alma practically screamed.

"Well, that's what he calls himself." Uncle Marcus sighed.

The girls sprinted upstairs, so fast they could barely breathe when they arrived at Tío Ramon's door. He and his wife, Aunt Dominique, were passing a crying Baby Richie back and forth, with lots of shushing and rocking.

"Oh, um, hi?" Alma said very quietly. She didn't know if maybe a loud voice would make the baby cry more.

"Alma! Del! Come in!" Aunt Dominique said.

"We could come back another time when Richie is a little, um, happier," Alma said.

"No, no, he'll calm down soon, I'm sure. Maybe one of you would like to hold him?"

Del and Alma exchanged a look. Neither of them knew anything about babies. Especially not crying babies. They wanted to hold their newest little cousin, but they also wanted to wait until he was sleeping, maybe. Sleeping babies seemed much easier to handle.

"We're actually here on a mission," Del said.

"A mysterious mission," Alma added.

"Ooooo, how exciting!" Aunt Dominique said. "I love a good mystery."

"Well, this one is about teacups," Alma explained. "Do you like mysteries about teacups?"

"Not the teacups," Tío Ramon said. "Not again."

"Again?" Del asked. "You've heard about teacups before?"

"Oh, ages ago. I don't even remember the details. My mother told us all about a tea set once—some big mistake, some broken, lost something-or-other. I don't know. I wish I remembered more but, well, hard to remember much of anything these days."

Alma wondered why a baby made it so hard to remember things, but when Baby Richie cried even louder, she almost forgot why they were here to begin with.

"Do you remember if you have one of the mystery teacups?" Alma asked.

Tío Ramon shrugged. "Who knows what we have around here," he said.

"We heard you're the king of Christmas," Del blurted out. "And we wondered if maybe it might be with your Christmas decorations."

"The king of Christmas," Tío Ramon repeated. "That's me. You girls want me to decorate your homes this year too? I know you usually just have a wreath out front, but maybe you'd like a singing Santa or my snowman with blinking lights instead? Something more magical."

Alma smiled. Abuelita would never let that happen. But Alma loved how magic was a little

different for everyone. "Maybe," she said. "But for now can we just check out the boxes?"

"Of course," Aunt Dominique said before Tío Ramon could suggest a giant reindeer or life-size nativity scene. "Check out the front closet."

Del's and Alma's hands shook with excitement as they looked in the closet. They were getting so close! They had six teacups already!

The whole closet was packed with decorations of every kind. Tío Ramon was right: it was

pretty magical. It took a while to dig through tinsel and strings of lights and ornaments of every size and shape and color, but finally they found a box with stockings. And one stocking had a Christmas tree stitched on the front.

Alma looked at Del.

Del looked at Alma.

They reached their hands in together and beamed when they touched the unmistakable handle of the seventh teacup.

"It's here!" Del said.

"One more to go!" Alma replied.

And with that, they kissed Baby Richie's now-smiling face and ran out the door to visit more family. It had been pretty easy and fun finding these seven cups. Surely the eighth cup would be a breeze to find!

Except there was one very big problem.

When they turned over the seventh teacup, there was nothing on the bottom.

9

Seven Cups

- Del -

Without any clues to go on, Del and Alma wandered Twenty-Third Avenue, stopping in to visit the rest of their relatives. Cousins and titis and friends who had become family over time. They were invited into homes and offered everything from chocolate milk to fruit salad to tostones. They talked about Baby Richie and Baby Louise, about what books and TV they liked and what was going on at school and what they were feeding Fraidycat these days. Del did not mention that she mostly fed Fraidycat broccoli under the table since Fraidycat liked everything, even Del's least-favorite vegetable.

They tried to talk about the mysterious tea set and the eighth teacup, but no one had anything to say on the matter. They either hadn't heard of the tea set or got very quiet when  it came up. Sometimes they would bring out a teacup that was pink striped or blue flowered or all wrong in some other way. But no one had the last sobbing-willow teacup.

"Why did the clues stop?" Alma asked. Her face was so sad. Del wanted to have an answer for her, a brilliant detective idea that would solve everything. But she didn't. Del was feeling pretty sad too.

By the time the sun was setting, Del and

Alma walked back down the street to their home. They picked up Evie on the way. She was sweaty and smiling after spending all afternoon at Titi Selma's home.

"First we made a swing set, then I learned how to make baby food, then I ate ice cream, and then I played in the swing set and it didn't break or anything, so I think I'm going to be a construction worker when I grow up. Or a swing set designer. Or maybe a mermaid astronaut. I haven't decided."

"Those are some really good options, Evie," Alma said.

"What about a mermaid construction worker?" Del asked.

"No, that's impossible," Evie said. "Mermaids can't build swing sets. Obviously."

"Oh," Del said, trying to figure out how mermaids could go into space. "Makes sense."

"Did you find all the teacups?" Evie asked.

"We have seven," Del said with a big sigh.

"We couldn't find the eighth one," Alma said with an even bigger sigh.

"Well, what's the new clue?" Evie asked.

Del showed her the bottom of the cup with nothing on it. Very quickly, even always-happy Evie frowned. No one knew what to say or do, and Del felt so disappointed. She'd wanted everything to come together perfectly. But then she remembered that that wasn't how magic worked. Magic wasn't about things being perfect. Magic was strange and unexpected and from the heart. It was messy. Only having seven cups when there were eight plates would be very messy.

"Hey, maybe seven cups is even more magical than eight!" Del said hopefully. "Let's go test it out!"

She marched her cousins right up to her room, where the rest of the tea set was hidden under her bed. She took out every last piece, and all of their newly found cups. She placed the plates and cups in a perfect circle and adjusted the one plate with no cup on top of it, as if the magic might appear right there.

"Magic!" Evie cried.

"Where?" Del asked.

"I'm trying to call for it. MAGIC! COME HERE!" Evie's voice boomed.

"I don't think that's how it works, Evie," Del said.

"Well, maybe we need something *in* the teapot?" Alma asked timidly.

"Great idea!" Del said. Sometimes Alma made things feel easy and clear. Something in the teapot! Of course! Del marched right to the bathroom and filled it up with water. The girls sat on Del's bedroom floor and waited for something to happen. Nothing did.

"Maybe . . . pour it into the cups?" Alma suggested.

"Yes!" Del said. "Of course!"

Del poured a little water into each teacup. They all peered inside. It was just water. It didn't bubble or sparkle or turn into diamonds or anything.

"I guess we could try drinking it?" Alma said, her eyebrows scrunched in concentration.

"Or pouring it on our heads," Evie said, sounding every bit as serious.

"Let's drink it," Del said. And they did. But it just tasted like water.

Alma's shoulders slumped. Evie's head hung. And Del's eyes filled with tears.

Without any clues, being a detective was very, very hard.

10

Vanilla, Lavender, and Chocolate

-Alma-

The next morning, over breakfast, Del wrote out a list of all kinds of things they could put in the teapot to make it magical.

"What's first?" Alma asked.

"The most magical liquid of all," Del said.

"Chocolate syrup?" Evie asked. "Oh! Or caramel syrup?"

"Nope," Del said, grinning.

"So I guess it's maple syrup?" Evie asked, a little disappointed.

"No, not syrup at all," Del said. Evie's face scrunched in confusion. "Bubble solution!"

"Bubble solution?" Alma said. "Like for blowing bubbles?"

"Yes!" Del said. She was getting more and more sure by the minute. "I mean it's clearly magical—it turns something normal into something beautiful. Isn't that what magic is?"

"I guess," Alma said.

Evie did not look convinced. She kept mumbling about all the different kinds of syrup—strawberry and peanut butter and even a weird white-chocolate one they'd had at a fancy ice cream shop once. All of those would be better than *bubbles*, Evie kept saying under her breath.

But Alma liked Del's idea, so the girls picked up bubble solution from Alma's home, and they brought it out to Abuelita's garden. Nothing happened when they poured it into the teapot. Nothing happened when they swirled it around.

Nothing happened when they poured it into the cups.

They went through the rest of Del's list. They tried filling the teapot with glitter. With Del's favorite passionfruit juice from the Venezuelan restaurant down the street. With air from the kitchen when Abuelita was cooking mofongo. Abuelita's cooking was always a little magical, after all, especially if plantains were involved. But still, nothing happened. They even listened to Evie and tried a combination of chocolate and maple syrups. All that did was make them sticky.

"So I know it's not very exciting, but what about tea?" Alma said at last. It sounded sort of silly, to suggest the most obvious thing in the world, but nothing was working, and she had to do *something*. "It's a teapot. Maybe it only works when it has tea."

Del's eyes lit up. So did Evie's. "Tea!" Del said. "Of course! Your mom is *always* drinking tea, Alma. She must have some we can use!"

The girls climbed back up the stairs all the way to Alma's top-floor apartment. And, magically, there was Alma's mother. Drinking a cup of tea.

"We need this!" Alma said, rushing toward her mother's cup.

"Whoa, watch out! It's hot!" her mother warned. "What do you need my tea for?"

"For magic," Alma said. Alma's mother smiled.

"Well, if it's for magic, then let me brew you a nice fresh pot," she said.

"Wait! It needs to be in our teapot!" Del said, running to get it.

"What do you think is more magical— lavender or vanilla?" Alma's mom said when Del returned.

"Lavender!" Alma said.

"Vanilla!" Del said.

"CHOCOLATE!" Evie cried.

"Well, in that case I'll put in one tea bag of lavender and one of vanilla," Alma's mom said. She didn't say anything about the chocolate. "How does that sound?"

"It sounds extremely magical," Alma said, wondering for the first time if her mother had some of the magic that her dad's side of the family had.

11

Watercolors, Trampolines, and Teacups

- Del -

Alma's mother put in a handful of ice cubes and brought the teapot downstairs for the girls. She made them promise to wait ten minutes before experimenting with it. Del had decided that they couldn't just wait around to see if the tea did anything. They'd have to *do something* with it. So they did. They drank it. They watered Titi Clara's roses with it. They rubbed it on their hands and into their hair. They brought Fraidy-cat over to a small puddle of it to see what she would do with it. She sniffed it, stuck a paw in it, and ran away.

Nothing magical had happened, except now Del, Alma, and Evie all smelled like lavender and vanilla. Which was very nice. But not magical at all.

"I guess the tea set won't be magical without that last teacup after all," Del said when they'd finished pouring tea on the lion statues that perched on the bottom of their stoop.

"I guess not," Alma agreed.

"You guys look sad!" someone called out from across the street. Alma and Evie looked up. Their friend June was just leaving the playground with her abuela and her little sister, Maggie.

"We are sad," Del said.

"Very sad," Alma agreed.

"Then come over and play!" June said. "I got new watercolors and a mini trampoline for my birthday last week. You want to check them out?

We can pretend to be Olympic gymnasts who are also famous artists!"

Alma and Del looked at each other. They weren't making any progress on the tea set. Yesterday's detective work had worn them out. And they did love painting. And jumping. And all of June's exciting imaginary ideas. "Sure!" they said in unison.

"Me too, me too!" Evie said.

"Make sure it's okay with your family," June's abuela said. She adjusted a shimmery scarf around her neck. She looked nervous. Or sad. Or both.

"I'll ask Abuelita!" Del exclaimed, getting up from the stoop.

"Oh. Well. Yes, okay," June's abuela said. Del noticed that she looked down and blushed. June's abuela and Abuelita had never been very close. Actually, Del couldn't remember a single time they'd spoken. And when Del asked if it would be okay to go to her home today, Abuelita looked out the window to see June and her abuela. She didn't wave. She just said that would be fine.

Alma and Del and Evie bounded back to the street, back to June and her abuela, ready for watercolors and trampolines and maybe forgetting about magic for a little bit.

But of course, they couldn't forget about magic. While Evie and Maggie played outside, June tried to talk about all kinds of other things—her new favorite movie and what color sneakers she should get and how pretty Del's voice was in music class. But Del just kept looking at Alma, wondering if she was trying to figure out the tea set too.

June brought out her new watercolors and

nice thick brushes and fancy, heavy paper. But Alma and Del both ended up painting teacups with sobbing-willow designs on them, and nothing else.

"Hey! My teacup!" June exclaimed when she looked away from her painting of Oscar, everyone's favorite neighborhood dog.

"No, it's our teacup," Del said.

"*No*," June said, rolling her eyes. "Look, it's definitely mine." June got up and went to the kitchen. When she returned, she was carrying the eighth sobbing-willow teacup.

Del and Alma gasped.

"The missing teacup!" Del exclaimed.

"It was here all along!" Alma gasped.

But June just looked very, very confused.

12

Teacup Tension, Family Fights

-Alma-

"What are you guys even talking about?" June asked. She held the teacup a little closer to herself, as if the girls might try to take it.

"Where did you get that teacup?" Del asked.

June smiled. "Oh, it's sort of a secret," she said. "It's a really special teacup. I promised I wouldn't talk about it."

"I'm sure you can just tell *us*," Alma said. "We're your friends!"

"Oh, well, I probably especially can't tell you," June said.

"What does that mean?" Del asked. "Come on, just tell us. You have to."

"Don't boss me around, Del. I don't have to do anything," June said. "Stop looking at my teacup."

"It's definitely not your teacup!" Del said. Alma tried to touch Del's shoulder to calm her down, but it didn't work. "It's ours! We have the whole set! We're just missing that one!"

"Well, if you don't have this one, that's because it's *mine*," June said. "You know, you're just like your abuela."

"What does that mean?" Alma asked. Usually, that would be the biggest compliment in the world. But something about the way June said it made her feel strange.

"My abuela said your abuela can't be trusted, and I don't think you can be either!" June said.

"Abuelita is the most trustworthy person in the world," Alma said, her voice a little louder than she expected it to be.

"Not according to my family!" June said.

"You are so wrong!" Del said. She seemed close to tears. Alma felt like crying too. Yesterday had already been so disappointing. And now they were getting into a terrible fight with their friend. And somehow the fight was about Abuelita!

"I want to go home," Alma said in a small voice.

"But she's being— She's saying— That's our teacup!"

Alma just shrugged. She hated all this fighting.

"Stop saying that about *my* teacup!" June cried.

"It's not yours!" Del yelled.

"Please, Del, can we just go?" Alma said again. And this time Del took a deep breath, looked right at her cousin, saw how upset she was, and slowly nodded.

This wasn't going the way it was supposed to be going. Not at all.

On their way out the door, Evie and Maggie stopped them.

"Hey! I heard you talking about the teacup!" Maggie said.

"You guys were loud," Evie said.

"Oh," Alma said, feeling a little sheepish.

"Yeah. Sorry we got into a fight with your sister."

"That's okay. I get into fights with her all the time!"

"I can see why," Del mumbled, but Alma elbowed her to be quiet.

"I don't know why everyone's always making a big deal out of that teacup," Maggie said. "Just because Abuela says it's magical! I've never seen it do any magic at all. So I don't know why we're supposed to keep it a big secret."

"She says it's magical?" Alma asked. Her heart pounded. She still wanted to leave, but they were so close to solving this magical mystery!

Maggie just shrugged. "That's what Abuela says, but I doubt it."

"It's definitely magical!" Evie said. "At least we think it is!"

"You've seen it do magic?" Maggie said. "Let me tell my sister!" Maggie rushed inside and came back out, dragging June along with her.

"June! They know how to make the teacup magical!"

"I doubt it," June said. "They don't know anything about *our* teacup."

"We're really good at magic!" Del said. "You know we are!"

"Everyone calm down," Alma said. "We have seven teacups, eight saucers, and a teapot. Maggie and June, you have a teacup that matches.

And we have to remember what Abuelita says. Magic only works if nothing is lost. If nothing is broken. This teacup has been lost. And something between our families is clearly broken. So what we need to do is work together."

"But—" June and Del said at the same time. Speaking in unison made them both smile a little, and Alma watched as their shoulders relaxed.

"Come on. We need the whole set for it to be magical. And we need each other for that, right?"

Del and June looked at each other.

"We have to at least try," Alma said.

"Fine," Del and June said again at the same time. Alma was almost positive she saw them smile even bigger, and maybe even start to laugh. Maybe they weren't getting along yet, but at least they'd all agreed on a plan.

13

Chocolate or Strawberries or Pineapple or Cake

- Del -

Everyone was quiet walking back to 86 ½ Twenty-Third Avenue. It was a good thing, Del thought. If they were being quiet, at least they weren't arguing with each other. Still, it was hard to think about the mean things June had said about Abuelita. Del thought everyone loved Abuelita as much as she did. Their neighborhood had always felt like one big family.

"Let's do this in the garden," Del said when they got home.

"Fine," June said.

"Yeah, fine," Maggie said.

"Yeah. Fine," Evie said, even though Evie was not mad at Del at all.

Del went upstairs to get the rest of the tea set, and Alma picked out a yellow-and-blue-striped picnic blanket for them to use. When everyone got settled, Del poured water into each cup, making sure not to spill or splash.

"I should get to sip first," June said.

"No, *I* should," Del said. "It's obviously my family's tea set, since we had most of it."

"I think we should all sip at the same time," Alma said. Del and June nodded. So did Maggie and Evie. Each girl held her cup gently and lifted it to her mouth. They each took a very small, timid sip, then put their cups back down. They looked at one another, everyone waiting for someone else to speak first.

"That's not water," Evie said at last.

"I put water in the teapot," Del said.

"But it tasted like chocolate!" Maggie said. "Like chocolate water."

"No, strawberries!" June declared.

"I thought it tasted like vanilla birthday cake," Evie said. "With sprinkles."

"No way," Del said. "It definitely tasted like cinnamon sugar. So delicious."

"Well, mine tasted like pineapple," Alma said. "Really, really yummy pineapple."

"Are you sure?" Del whispered to Alma. "You didn't taste cinnamon sugar?"

Alma shook her head. "Let's try again," she said. And they did.

Everyone's sips were bigger this time. More excited. And when they put their cups back down, they were all grinning.

"Still cinnamon-sugary!" Del said, bouncing a little.

"Mine's still strawberry," June said.

Each time they sipped from the cups, they smiled bigger and brighter. Soon they were all beaming and starting to giggle.

"This is so cool!" Alma said. "It's like, I know it's water, but it's also sort of not water!"

"Yes! Strawberries are my favorite, and this has the perfect strawberry taste," June said.

"It's so weird!" Maggie said.

"And fun!" Evie said.

"And magical," Del said.

"Super magical," June said.

The delicious magical tea made the afternoon sun feel sunnier and the blanket feel cozier and the day feel better. And it made their friendship feel magical too. They'd forgotten all about their fight, all about their families not getting along. Soon they were laughing so loudly that Abuelita must have overheard them.

"Girls! What's all the noise about? You woke me and Fraidycat from our afternoon nap!"

Abuelita said, and as she walked out to join them in the garden, she saw her grandchildren. Their friends. And of course, the tea set.

"Oh!" Abuelita said.

Del tried to figure out the look on Abuelita's face. A little confused. A little surprised.

And maybe a little upset too.

The Truth

-Alma-

Abuelita looked like she needed a moment to catch her breath. So Alma and her cousins and friends stayed quiet. And still. And nervous.

"Is she mad?" Maggie whispered to Evie.

"I don't know," Evie said. "I've never seen Abuelita mad. Abuelita, are you mad?"

"I'm . . . well . . . I'm . . . What is going on here? And how are you all—? Where did all these cups come from? It looks like maybe you have all, um, eight of the cups here."

Alma nodded. She didn't want to upset Abuelita, but she knew not to lie. "We went looking for them. And, well, we found them. You said the tea set was incomplete, and we wanted to complete it. So that the magic wasn't lost anymore."

"Ah," Abuelita said. And the look on her face changed. She didn't look maybe-mad anymore. Now she looked sad. Very sad.

"And it's not lost!" Del said. "We found it! We found the tea set and we found the magic, and just like always, magic is bringing everyone together!"

"I can see that," Abuelita said.

Alma watched as she looked from person to person.

"You do look happy," Abuelita said. "And magic does bring people together. Es verdad."

"It really *is* true, Abuelita," Alma said. "This tea set and its magic made us all friends again."

Abuelita gave an Abuelita shrug. "Could I have a cup of magic too?"

"We would love that!" Del said.

June grabbed the teapot and poured a cup for Abuelita. And Abuelita sat. And sipped. And smiled at whatever her magical tea tasted like.

"It's time to be honest," Abuelita said. "Magic makes friendship. And it makes togetherness. And it also makes us tell the truth. You deserve to know the truth."

"What truth?" Alma asked.

"About this very tea set," Abuelita said. "The truth is, I made this tea set with my very best friend. We decorated it with a drawing of our favorite tree in the world. The sobbing willow. And the first time we used it, my friend tasted pumpkins and clove. And I tasted extra-sugary lavender lemonade. And it was then that we knew it was magical. I was very young. Very young and new to the city and scared that there wasn't enough magic to go around. I was scared of a lot of things. And fear can make you do some strange things. Terrible things." Abuelita looked down at her teacup. She sighed. Alma thought she even saw her wipe away a tear.

"What did you do?" Del asked.

"I wanted the magic all to myself, mi cielo," Abuelita said. "I thought that's what I needed, so I took all those beautiful cups, and hid them with all my different family members and told my friend she could only keep one for herself. I left some clues behind as the homes and cups switched hands over the years, so that I would know where the teacups were when I needed them. I asked them to keep my secret for me. I thought having that secret would mean that I was the most magical, my family was the most magical, and that being the most magical would make me safe in this new place. This new place that was my home and also sometimes didn't feel like my home. I missed Puerto Rico and I also knew I belonged here, but some days people acted like I didn't, and it was very confusing. But I was so, so wrong to take all that magic for myself. And it didn't make me safe. Or magical. It only made me embarrassed. And sad. And missing my old friend. But too scared to fix things."

"I didn't know you'd ever made any mistakes," Alma said, shocked.

"Especially such a big mistake," Evie said. "That's a *really* big mistake."

Abuelita smiled a sad smile. "It was a really, really big mistake," she said. "And I bet you can guess who that very special best friend of mine was."

Abuelita looked at June and Maggie extra long. Their eyes widened.

"Our abuela?" June asked.

"Your wonderful abuela," Abuelita replied.

15

Better Than Magic

-Del-

Del was astonished. Abuelita had told her many, many stories over the years. But never one like this. Usually, in Abuelita's stories, Abuelita was making good decisions, being kind and smart and sweet to everyone. But this time, Abuelita's story was about a very big mistake.

"Why didn't you just apologize?" Del asked.

"I was ashamed," Abuelita said. "And being ashamed is one of the hardest feelings there is.

It's a feeling that makes it hard for you to do the right thing."

"Are you still ashamed?" Del asked.

"A little," Abuelita said. "But seeing you girls out here, experiencing the beautiful magic of tea parties and friendship, makes me want to fix things. I miss my friend."

"I bet she misses you too," June said.

"Do you think so?" Abuelita asked. Del had never seen this side of Abuelita before. It reminded her, well, a little of herself. When she fought with Alma or someone at school, or even June today, she felt nervous that she'd never be able to fix it, and scared that that person wouldn't ever like her again. She felt embarrassed. She could see how that would make her want to run away and hide.

"Abuela forgives me when I mess up," Maggie said. "She says it's all a part of growing up."

"Are you still growing up, Abuelita?" Evie asked.

Abuelita gave an Abuelita shrug. Followed by a big Abuelita smile. "I suppose I am," she said at last. "And I suppose I know what to do after all." And with that, Abuelita stood up, her teacup in one hand, grabbing the teapot with the other. "Del, take the blanket. Alma, Evie, make sure we have all the cups and plates, por favor."

The girls did as they were told. Abuelita led the way, her head high, a nervous smile on her face, the girls following behind.

Abuelita led the girls around to the front of the house and down the street, past their cousins' and titis' and tíos' homes. Past the park and the sobbing willow and Oscar on a walk with Cora and Javi. Past Felix drawing with chalk outside his home and Cassie peering out her kitchen window. Past the bakery with the best croissants and the library with the coziest chairs and the tiny Italian restaurant with the twirliest spaghetti.

People glanced at the tea-party parade, smiling at their perfectly balanced cups and maybe the smell of the tea—whatever it smelled like to each of them.

Abuelita and the girls walked all through the neighborhood, until they got to the blue door of the home where June and Maggie lived with their abuela.

Their abuela came to the door. She had a flower pinned in her hair and sparkly purple eye shadow and a polka-dotted dress and a confused look on her face. Del saw exactly why Abuelita was friends with her. She was so clearly magical and fun and kind and wise just like Abuelita.

"Maria," Abuelita said. "I brought you a tea party. With our tea set."

Something about the word *our* made June's abuela's face relax.

"Gabriella," June's abuela said back. "I'm very surprised to see you. To see all of you."

"I hope you will join me for a cup of tea," Abuelita said.

June's abuela paused. She looked like she might cry or laugh or faint. "Only if it tastes like pumpkins and clove," she said, and smiled.

"Or extra-sugary lavender lemonade," Abuelita said in return.

June's abuela smiled even bigger.

"Would you like to come inside?" she asked.

"I think your front yard would be a perfect spot, actually," Abuelita said. She tapped on Del's shoulder to tell her to put down the blanket. Then Abuelita sat right down on it and poured June's abuela a cup of tea. "I am so, so sorry," Abuelita said. "I hope you can forgive me. I made a big mistake. And I made an even bigger mistake in not fixing it much sooner."

June's abuela nodded. She took a sip of tea. Del wondered if it tasted like pumpkins and clove, or something else entirely. "Oh, Gabriella," June's abuela said after two more big, smiling sips. "Sometimes it takes a long time to fix what is broken. All that matters is that it gets fixed, eventually. All is forgiven."

Abuelita and June's abuela rose and gave each other a huge hug. It made everyone smile. Del was so happy they had fixed things. And she was also a little happy to have learned that Abuelita made mistakes. Magical, wonderful, practically perfect Abuelita had made a big mistake that she hadn't known how to fix.

But eventually, with everyone's help, she had been able to make it right.

It made Del feel hopeful and happy and proud.

"I wish everyone in the neighborhood could have a taste of the magical tea," Alma said.

"I want to know what it would taste like to all our neighbors."

"Well, why can't they?" Del asked.

"Well, first of all, we don't have enough

teacups," Alma said. "And second of all, wouldn't it be weird to go around offering everyone tea?"

Abuelita shrugged her Abuelita shrug. So did Evie. Then Del. Then June and Maggie and June's abuela. It looked a little different, each time someone new did it.

"I think now that all the cups are together and our friendship has been repaired, the magic may be strong enough for everyone to use their own cups," Abuelita said. "What do you think, Maria?"

"I bet you're right," June's abuela said. "Magic grows. And changes. And breaks and then gets stronger when it's fixed."

"Like hearts," Abuelita said in a quiet voice that Del had never heard before.

"Sí," June's abuela said. "Like hearts."

And with that, Evie leaped up from the blanket and sprinted down the street to where Cassie lived. Del and Alma couldn't hear what she was saying, but they could see her enthusiastic hand gestures and her bouncing knees. Cassie vanished for a moment, then reappeared, one hand holding a yellow teacup, the other being pulled by Evie.

Alma didn't hesitate. She got right up and poured her a cup.

Cassie made a dreamy face at the taste of her tea, and Del and Alma knew they had to bring absolutely everyone into the magic. So off they went, to knock on the doors of their family members and friends, the shop owners and dog walkers and even the neighbors they didn't know well at all. Soon the picnic blanket was too crowded, so more blankets were brought out, with more teacups in all shapes and sizes and colors.

"It tastes like banana cream pie!" someone exclaimed.

"No, it tastes like chocolate chip cookies," someone else said.

"It tastes like my mother's carrot-ginger soup," someone else insisted.

Del was sure everyone's tea was delicious. But even better than that was the way it felt

to be together, sharing magic. Letting it change.
Watching it grow.

Del squeezed next to Alma. "This is pretty
cool," she said to her best-friend-cousin.

"This is *everything*," Alma said, leaning her head on Del's shoulder.

And it was.

Acknowledgments

This series is a joy to write, a happy place in tough moments, and a piece of my heart, as well as a piece of my family. Thank you to everyone who helped make it happen, every step of the way.

Thank you, Luisa Uribe, for the many beautiful and intricate and magical ways your illustrations told the story of this family. I smile at every surprising and sweet moment you capture.

Thank you, Mabel Hsu, for your clarity, your sense of joy, and your tireless work here and everywhere. You are such a trusted and inspiring presence.

Thank you, Victoria Marini, for always being a safe and steady force in my world.

Thank you, Tanu Srivastava, for your smart questions, deep dedication, and all the profound and far-reaching work you do.

Thank you to Katherine Tegen for making sure these books found their way onto shelves and into homes. And thank you to the entire Katherine Tegen Books team for making such beautiful books and helping me tell the stories of my heart. Thank you especially David L. DeWitt, Lena Reilly, Amy Ryan, Alexandra Rakaczki, Maya Myers, Sean Cavanagh, Vanessa Nuttry, and Emma Meyer.

Thank you to my entire family—from NYC, New England, Wisconsin, Chicago, Puerto Rico, Ireland, and beyond. You are all in these pages.

And thank you, Alex Arnold, for one day of many at a café, helping me find magic.